SECRET SEVEN
ADVENTURE

Enid Blyton's
Secret Seven Adventure

Illustrated by W.F.P.

AWARD PUBLICATIONS LIMITED

ISBN 0-86163-532-9

Text copyright © Darrell Waters Limited
Illustrations copyright © 1991 Award Publications Limited

Enid Blyton's signature is a trademark of Darrell Waters Limited

First published 1950 by Hodder and Stoughton

This edition first published by
Award Publications Limited, Spring House,
Spring Place, Kentish Town, London NW5 3BH

Photoset by Rowland Phototypesetting Limited
Bury St Edmunds, Suffolk

Printed in Hungary

Contents

One

A Secret Seven meeting

THE Secret Seven Society was having its usual weekly meeting. Its meeting place was down in the old shed at the bottom of the garden belonging to Peter and Janet. On the door were the letters S.S. painted in green.

Peter and Janet were in the shed, waiting. Janet was squeezing lemons into a big jug, making lemonade for the meeting. On a plate lay seven ginger biscuits and one big dog biscuit.

That was for Scamper, their golden spaniel. He sat with his eyes on the plate, as if he was afraid his biscuit might jump off and disappear!

'Here come the others,' said Peter, looking out of the window. 'Yes – Colin – George – Barbara – Pam – and Jack. And you and I make the Seven.'

'Woof,' said Scamper, feeling left out.

'Sorry, Scamper,' said Peter. 'But you're not a member – just a hanger-on – but a very *nice* one!'

Bang! Somebody knocked at the door.

'Password, please,' called Peter. He never un-locked the door until the person outside said the password.

'Rabbits!' said Colin, and Peter unlocked the door. 'Rabbits!' said Jack, and 'Rabbits,' said the others in turn. That was the very latest password. The Secret Seven altered the word every week, just in *case* anyone should get to hear of it.

Peter looked at everyone keenly as they came in and sat down. 'Where's your badge, Jack?' he asked.

Jack looked uncomfortable. 'I'm awfully sorry,' he said, 'but I think Susie's got it. I hid it in my drawer, and it was gone when I looked for it this morning. Susie's an awful pest when she likes.'

Susie was Jack's sister. She badly wanted to belong to the Society, but as Jack kept patiently pointing out, as long as there were Seven in the Secret Seven, there couldn't possibly be any more.

'Susie needs shaking,' said Peter. 'You'll have to get back the badge somehow, Jack, and then in future don't hide it in a drawer or anywhere, but pin it on to your pyjamas at night and wear it. Then Susie can't get it.'

'Right,' said Jack. He looked round to see if everyone else was wearing a badge. Yes – each

member had a little round button with the letters
S.S. neatly worked on it. He felt very annoyed with
Susie.

'Has anyone anything exciting to report?' asked
Peter, handing round the seven ginger biscuits. He
tossed Scamper the big dog biscuit, and the spaniel
caught it deftly in his mouth. Soon everyone was
crunching and munching.

Nobody had anything to report at all. Barbara
looked at Peter.

'This is the fourth week we've had nothing to
report, and nothing has happened,' she said. 'It's
very dull. I don't see much point in having a Secret
Society if it doesn't *do* something – solve some
mystery or have an adventure.'

'Well, think one up, then,' said Peter, promptly.
'You seem to think mysteries and adventures grow
on trees, Barbara.'

Janet poured out the lemonade. '*I* wish something exciting would happen, too,' she said. 'Can't
we make up some kind of adventure, just to go on
with?'

'What sort?' asked Colin. 'Oooh, this lemonade's
sour!'

'I'll put some more honey in,' said Janet. 'Well,
I mean, couldn't we dress up as Red Indians or

something, and go somewhere and stalk people without their knowing it? We've got some lovely Red Indian clothes, Peter and I.'

They talked about it for a while. They discovered that between them they had six sets of Red Indian clothes.

'Well, I know what we'll do, then,' said George. 'We'll dress up, and go off to Little Thicket. We'll split into two parties, one at each end of the thicket – and we'll see which party can stalk and catch Colin – he's the only one without a Red Indian dress. That'll be fun.'

'I don't much want to be stalked by all six of you,' said Colin. 'I hate being jumped on all at once.'

'It's only a game!' said Janet. 'Don't be silly.'

'Listen – there's somebody coming!' said Peter. Footsteps came up the path right to the shed. There was a tremendously loud bang at the door, which made everyone jump.

'Password!' said Peter, forgetting that all the Secret Seven were there.

'Rabbits!' was the answer.

'It's *Susie*!' said Jack in a rage. He flung open the door, and there, sure enough, was his cheeky sister, wearing the S.S. button, too!

'I'm a member!' she cried. 'I know the password and I've got the badge!'

Everyone got up in anger, and Susie fled, giggling as she went. Jack was scarlet with rage.

'I'm going after her,' he said. 'And now we'll have to think of a new password, too!'

'The password can be Indians!' Peter called after him. 'Meet here at half-past two!'

Two

A Red Indian afternoon

AT half-past two the Seven Society arrived by ones and twos. Jack arrived first, wearing his badge again. He had chased and caught Susie, and taken it from her.

'I'll come and bang at the door again and shout the password,' threatened Susie.

'That won't be any good,' said Jack.

'We've got a new one!'

Everyone said the new password cautiously, just in *case* that tiresome Susie was anywhere about.

'Indians!'

'Indians!' The password was whispered time after time till all seven were gathered together. Everyone had brought Red Indian suits and head-dresses. Soon they were all dressing, except Colin, who hadn't one.

'Now off we go to Little Thicket,' said Peter, prancing about with a most terrifying-looking hatchet. Fortunately, it was only made of wood. 'I'll take Janet and Jack for my two men, and George can have Barbara and Pam. Colin's to be the one we both try to stalk and capture.'

'No tying me to trees and shooting off arrows at me,' said Colin, firmly. 'That's fun for you, but not for me. See?'

They had all painted their faces in weird patterns, except Colin. Jack had a rubber knife which he kept pretending to plunge into Scamper. They really did look a very fierce collection of Indians indeed.

They set off for Little Thicket, which was about half a mile away, across the fields. It lay beside a big mansion called Milton Manor, which had high walls all round it.

'Now, what we'll do is to start out at opposite ends of Little Thicket,' said Peter. 'My three can take this end, and you three can take the other end, George. Colin can go to the middle. We'll all shut our eyes and count one hundred – and then we'll begin to hunt for Colin and stalk him.'

'And if I spot any of you and call your name, you have to get up and show yourselves,' said Colin. 'You'll be out of the game then.'

'And if any one of us manages to get right up to you and pounce on you, then you're his prisoner,' said Peter. 'Little Thicket is just the right kind of place for this!'

It certainly was. It was a mixture of heather and bushes and trees. Big, heathery tufts grew there, and patches of wiry grass, small bushes, and big and little trees. There were plenty of places to hide, and anyone could stalk a person from one end of the thicket to the other without being seen, if he crawled carefully along on his tummy.

The two parties separated, and went to each end of Little Thicket. A fence bounded one side and on the other the walls of Milton Manor grounds rose strong and high. If Colin could manage to get out of either end of Little Thicket uncaptured, he would be clever!

He went to stand in the middle, waiting for the others to count their hundred with their eyes shut. As soon as Peter waved a handkerchief to show that the counting had begun, Colin ran to a tree. He climbed quickly up into the thick branches, and sat himself on a broad bough. He grinned.

'They can stalk me all they like, from one end of the thicket to the other, but they won't find me!' he thought. 'And when they're all tired of looking and give up, I'll shin down and stroll up to them!'

The counting was up. Six Red Indians began to

spread out and worm their way silently through heather and thick undergrowth and long grass.

Colin could see where some of them were by the movement of the undergrowth. He kept peeping between the boughs of his tree, chuckling to himself. This was fun!

And then something very surprising caught his eye. He glanced over to the high wall that surrounded the grounds of Milton Manor, and saw that somebody was astride the top! Even as he looked the man jumped down and disappeared from view, and Colin heard the crackling of undergrowth. Then everything was still. Colin couldn't see him at all. He was most astonished. What had the man been doing, climbing over the wall?

Colin couldn't for the life of him think what was best to do. He couldn't start yelling to the others from the tree. Then he suddenly saw that Peter, or one of the others, was very near where the man had gone to ground!

It was Peter. He had thought he had heard somebody not far from him, and he had felt sure it was Colin, squirming his way along. So he squirmed in that direction too.

Ah! He was sure there was somebody hiding in the middle of that bush! It was a great gorse bush, in full bloom. It must be Colin hiding there.

Cautiously Peter wriggled on his tummy right up to the bush. He parted the brown stems, and gazed in amazement at the man there. It wasn't Colin, after all!

As for the man, he was horrified. He suddenly saw a dreadful, painted face looking at him through the bush, and saw what he thought was a real hatchet aimed at him. He had no idea it was only wood!

He got up at once and fled – and for a moment Peter was so amazed that he didn't even follow!

Three

A shock for Colin

By the time Peter had stood up to see where the horrified man had gone, he had completely disappeared. There wasn't a sign of him anywhere.

'Bother!' said Peter, vexed. 'Fat lot of good I am as a Red Indian. Can't even stalk somebody right under my nose. Where in the world has the fellow gone?'

He began to hunt here and there, and soon the others, seeing him standing up, knew that something had happened. They called to him.

'Peter – what is it? Why are you showing yourself?'

'There was a man hiding under one of the bushes,' said Peter. 'I just wondered why. But he got up and shot away. Anyone see where he went?'

No one had seen him at all. They clustered round Peter, puzzled. 'Fancy – seven of us crawling hidden in this field – and not one saw the man run off,' said Pam. 'We haven't even seen Colin!'

'The game's finished for this afternoon,' said Peter. He didn't want anyone else to come suddenly on the man in hiding – it would give them such a fright. 'We'll call Colin.'

So they yelled for him. 'Colin! Come out, wherever you are! The game's finished.'

They waited for him suddenly to stand up and appear. But he didn't. There was no answer to their call, and no Colin suddenly appeared.

'Colin!' yelled everyone. 'Come on out.'

Still he didn't come. He didn't even shout back. It was odd.

'Don't be funny!' shouted George. 'The game's over! Where are you?'

Colin was where he had been all the time – hidden up in his tree. Why didn't he shout back? Why didn't he shin down the tree and race over to the others, pleased that he hadn't been caught?

He didn't show himself for a very good reason. He was much too frightened!

He had had a shock when he saw the man drop down from the wall, and run to the thicket and hide – and he had an even greater shock when he saw him suddenly appear from a nearby bush, and run to the foot of the tree that he himself was hiding in.

Then he heard the sounds of someone clambering

up at top speed – good gracious, the man was climbing the very tree that Colin himself had chosen for a hiding place!

Colin's heart beat fast. He didn't like this at all. What would the man say if he suddenly climbed up on top of him? He would certainly be very much annoyed.

The man came steadily up. But when he was almost up to the branch on which Colin sat, he stopped. The branch wasn't strong enough to hold a man, though it was quite strong enough for a boy.

The man curled himself up in a fork of the tree just below Colin. He was panting hard, but trying to keep his breathing as quiet as possible. Peter was not so very far away and might hear it.

Colin sat as if he was turned to stone. Who was this man? Why had he come over the wall? Why had he hidden in Little Thicket? He would never have done that if he had known it was full of the Secret Seven playing at Red Indians!

And now here he was up Colin's tree, still in hiding – and at any moment he might look up and see Colin. It was very unpleasant indeed.

Then Colin heard the others shouting for him. 'Colin! Come out, wherever you are – the game's finished!'

But poor Colin didn't dare to come out, and certainly didn't dare to shout back. He hardly dared to breathe, and hoped desperately that he wouldn't have to sneeze or cough. He sat there as still as a mouse, waiting to see what would happen.

The man also sat there as still as a mouse, watching the six children below, peering at them through the leaves of the tree. Colin wished they had brought old Scamper with them. He would have sniffed the man's tracks and gone to the foot of the tree!

But Scamper had been left behind. He always got much too excited when they were playing Red Indians, and by his barking gave away where everyone was hiding!

After the others had hunted for Colin and called him, they began to walk off. 'He must have escaped us and gone home,' said Peter. 'Well, we'll go too. We can't find that man, and I don't know that I want to, either. He looked a nasty bit of work to me.'

In despair, Colin watched them leave Little Thicket and disappear down the field-path. The man saw them go too. He gave a little grunt and slid down the tree.

Colin had been able to see nothing of him except the top of his head and his ears. He could still see nothing of the man as he made his way cautiously out of the thicket. He was a far, far better Red Indian than any of the Secret Seven, that was certain!

And now – was it safe for Colin to get down? He certainly couldn't stay up in the tree all night!

Four

Is it an adventure?

COLIN slid down the tree. He stood at the foot, looking warily round. Nobody was in sight. The man had completely vanished.

'I'll run at top speed and hope for the best,' thought Colin, and off he went. Nobody stopped him! Nobody yelled at him. He felt rather ashamed of himself when he came to the field-path and saw the cows staring at him in surprise.

He went back to the farmhouse where Peter and Janet lived. Maybe the Secret Seven were still down in the shed, stripped of their Red Indian things and wiping the paint off their faces.

He ran down the path to the shed. The door was shut as usual. The S.S. showed up well with the two letters painted so boldly. There was the sound of voices from inside the shed.

Colin knocked. 'Let me in!' he cried. 'I'm back too.'

There was a silence. The door didn't open. Colin

banged again impatiently. 'You know it's only me. Open the door!'

Still it didn't open. And Colin remembered. He must give the password, of course! What in the world was it? Thankfully he remembered it, as he caught a glimpse of brilliant Red Indian feathers through the shed-window.

'Indians!' he shouted.

The door opened. 'And now *every*body in the district knows our latest password,' said Peter's voice in disgust. 'We'll have to choose another. Come in. Wherever have you been? We yelled and yelled for you at Little Thicket.'

'I know. I heard you,' said Colin, stepping inside. 'I say, I'm sorry I shouted out the password like that. I wasn't thinking. But I've got some news – most peculiar news!'

'What?' asked everyone, and stopped rubbing the paint from their faces.

'You know when Peter stood up and shouted out that he'd found a man in hiding, don't you?' said Colin. 'Well, I was quite nearby – as a matter of fact, I was up a tree!'

'Cheat!' said George. 'That's not playing Red Indians!'

'Who said it wasn't?' demanded Colin. 'I bet Red

Indians climbed trees as well as wriggling on their tummies. Anyway, I was up that tree – and, will you believe it, the man that Peter found came running up to my tree, and climbed it too!'

'Wow!' said George. 'What did you do?'

'Nothing,' said Colin. 'He didn't come up quite as far as I was – so I just sat tight, and didn't make a sound. I saw him before Peter did, actually. I saw him on the top of the wall that surrounds Milton Manor – then he dropped down, ran to the thicket and disappeared.'

'What happened in the end?' asked Janet, excited.

'After you'd all gone, he slid down the tree and went,' said Colin. 'I didn't see him any more. I slid down too, and ran for home. I felt a bit scared, actually.'

'Whatever was he doing, behaving like that?' wondered Jack. 'What was he like?'

'Well, I only saw the top of his head and his ears,' said Colin. 'Did *you* see him closely, Peter?'

'Yes, fairly,' said Peter. 'But he wasn't anything out of the ordinary really – clean-shaven, dark-haired – nothing much to remember him by.'

'Well, I suppose that's the last we'll hear of him,' said Barbara. 'The adventure that passed us by! We shall never know exactly what he was doing, and why.'

'He spoilt our afternoon, anyway,' said Pam. 'Not that we'd have caught Colin – hiding up a tree like that. We'll have to make a rule that trees are not to be climbed when we're playing at stalking.'

'When's our next meeting – and are we going to have a new password?' asked Janet.

'We'll meet on Wednesday evening,' said Peter. 'Keep your eyes and ears open for anything exciting or mysterious or adventurous, as usual. It *is* a pity we didn't capture that man – or find out more about him. I'm sure he was up to no good.'

'What about a password?' asked Janet again.

'Well – we'll have "Adventure", I think,' said Peter. 'Seeing we've just missed one!'

They all went their several ways home – and, except for Colin, nobody thought much more of the peculiar man at Little Thicket. But the radio that evening suddenly made all the Secret Seven think of him again!

'Lady Lucy Thomas's magnificent and unique pearl necklace was stolen from her bedroom at Milton Manor this afternoon,' said the announcer. 'Nobody saw the thief, or heard him, and he got away in safety.' Peter and Janet sprang up at once.

'That's the man we saw!' yelled Peter. 'Would you believe it! Call a meeting of the Secret Seven for tomorrow, Janet – this is an adventure again!'

Five

An important meeting

THAT night the Secret Seven were very excited. Janet and Peter had slipped notes into everyone's letterbox. 'Meeting at half-past nine. IMPORTANT! S.S.S.'

Colin and George had no idea at all what was up, because they hadn't listened to the radio. But the others had all heard of the theft of Lady Lucy Thomas's necklace, and, knowing that she lived by Little Thicket, they guessed that the meeting was to be about finding the thief!

At half-past nine the Society met. Janet and Peter were ready for them in the shed. Raps at the door came steadily. 'Password!' called Peter, sternly, each time.

'Adventure!' said everyone in a low voice. 'Adventure!' 'Adventure!' One after another the members were admitted to the shed.

'Where's that awful sister of yours – Susie?' Peter asked Jack. 'I hope she's not about anywhere. This is a really important meeting today. Got your badge?'

'Yes,' said Jack. 'Susie's gone out for the day. Anyway, she doesn't know our latest password.'

'What's the meeting about?' asked Colin. 'I know something's up by the look on Janet's face. She looks as if she's going to burst!'

'*You'll* feel like bursting when you know,' said Janet. 'Because you're going to be rather important, seeing that you and Peter are the only ones who saw the thief we're going after.'

Colin and George looked blank. They didn't know what Janet was talking about, of course. Peter soon explained.

'You know the fellow that Colin saw yesterday, climbing over the wall that runs round Milton Manor?' said Peter. 'The one *I* saw hiding in the bush – and then he went and climbed up into the very tree Colin was hiding in? Well, it said on the radio last night that a thief had got into Lady Lucy Thomas's bedroom and taken her magnificent pearl necklace.'

'Gracious!' said Pam, with a squeal. 'And that was the man you and Colin saw!'

'Yes,' said Peter. 'It must have been. And now the thing is – what do we do about it? This is an adventure – if only we can find that man – and if *only* we could find the necklace too – that would be a fine feather in the cap of the Secret Seven.'

There was a short silence. Everyone was thinking hard. 'But how can we find him?' asked Barbara at last. 'I mean – only you and Colin saw him, Peter – and then just for a moment.'

'And don't forget that *I* only saw the top of his head and tips of his ears,' said Colin. 'I'd like to know how I could possibly know anyone from those things. Anyway, I can't go about looking at the tops of people's heads!'

Janet laughed. 'You'd have to carry a stepladder about with you!' she said, and that made everyone else laugh too.

'Oughtn't we to tell the police?' asked George.

'I think we ought,' said Peter, considering the matter carefully. 'Not that we can give them any help at all, really. Still – that's the first thing to be done. Then maybe we could help the police, and, anyway, we could snoop round and see if we can find out anything on our own.'

'Let's go down to the police station now,' said George. 'That would be an exciting thing to do! Won't the inspector be surprised when we march in, all seven of us!'

They left the shed and went down to the town. They trooped up the steps of the police station, much to the astonishment of the young policeman inside.

'Can we see the inspector?' asked Peter. 'We've got some news for him – about the thief that stole Lady Lucy's necklace.'

The inspector had heard the clatter of so many feet and he looked out of his room. 'Hello, *hello!*' he said, pleased. 'The Secret Seven again! And what's the password this time?'

Nobody told him, of course, Peter grinned.

'We just came to say we saw the thief climb over the wall of Milton Manor yesterday,' he said. 'He hid in a bush first and then in a tree where Colin was hiding. But that's about all we know!'

The inspector soon got every single detail from the Seven, and he looked very pleased. 'What beats me is how the thief climbed that enormous wall!' he said. 'He must be able to climb like a cat. There was no ladder used. Well, Secret Seven, there's nothing much you can do, I'm afraid, except keep your eyes open in case you see this man again.'

'The only thing is – Colin only saw the top of his head, and I only caught a quick glimpse of him, and he looked so very, *very* ordinary,' said Peter. 'Still you may be sure we'll do our best!'

Off they all went again down the steps into the street. 'And *now*,' said Peter, 'we'll go to the place where Colin saw the man getting over the wall. We just *might* find something there – you never know!'

Six

Some peculiar finds

THE Seven made their way to Little Thicket, where they had played their game of Red Indians the day before.

'Now, where exactly did you say that the man climbed over?' Peter asked Colin. Colin considered. Then he pointed to a holly tree.

'See that holly? Well – he came over the wall between that tree and the little oak. I'm pretty certain that was exactly the place.'

'Come on, then – we'll go and see,' said Peter. Feeling really rather important, the Seven walked across Little Thicket and came to the place between the holly tree and the little oak. They stood and gazed up at the wall.

It was at least ten or eleven feet high. How could anyone climb a sheer wall like that without even a ladder?

'Look – here's where he leapt down,' said Pam, suddenly, and she pointed to a deep mark in the ground near the holly tree. They all looked.

'Yes – that must have been where his feet landed,' said George. 'Pity we can't tell anything from the mark – I mean, if it had been footprints, for instance, it would have helped a lot. But it's only just a deep mark – probably made by his heels.'

'I wish we could go to the other side of the wall,' said Peter, suddenly. 'We might perhaps find a footprint or two there. Let's go and ask the gardener if we can go into the grounds. He's a friend of our cow-man and he knows me.'

'Good idea,' said George, so off they all went again. The gardener was working inside the front garden, beyond the great iron gates. The children called to him, and he looked up.

'Mr Johns!' shouted Peter. 'Could we come in and snoop round? About the thief, you know. We saw him climb over the wall, and the inspector of police has asked us to keep our eyes open. So we're looking round.'

Mr Johns grinned. He opened the gates. 'Well, if I come with you, I don't reckon you can do much harm,' he said. 'Beats me how that thief climbed those walls. I was working here in the front garden all yesterday afternoon, and if he'd come in at the gates I'd have seen him. But he didn't.'

The seven children went round the walls with Mr Johns. Colin saw the top of the holly tree and the top of the little nearby oak jutting above the wall. He stopped.

'This is where he climbed up,' he said. 'Now let's look for footprints.'

There were certainly marks in the earth – but no footprints.

The Seven bent over the marks.

'Funny, aren't they?' said Peter, puzzled. 'Quite round and regular – and about three inches across – as if someone had been pounding about with a large-sized broom handle – hammering the end of it into the ground. What could have made these marks, Mr Johns?'

'Beats me,' said Mr Johns, also puzzled. 'Maybe the police will make something of them, now they know you saw the thief climb over the wall just here.'

Everyone studied the round, regular marks again. There seemed no rhyme or reason for them at all. They looked for all the world as if someone had been stabbing the ground with the tip of a broom handle or something – and why should any-one do that? And anyway, if they did, how would it help them to climb over a wall?

'There's been no ladder used, that I *can* say,' said Mr Johns. 'All mine are locked up in a shed – and there they all are still – and the key's in my pocket. How that fellow climbed this steep wall, I can't think.'

'He must have been an acrobat, that's all,' said Janet looking up to the top of the wall. Then she spotted something, and pointed to it in excitement.

'Look – what's that – caught on that sharp bit of brick there – half-way up?'

Everybody stared. 'It looks like a bit of wool,' said Pam at last. 'Perhaps, when the thief climbed up, that sharp bit caught his clothes, and a bit of wool was pulled out.'

'Help me up, George,' ordered Peter. 'I'll get it. It might be a very valuable clue.'

George hoisted him up, and Peter made a wild grab at the piece of wool. He got it, and George let him down to the ground again. They all gathered round to look at it.

It was really rather ordinary – just a bit of blue wool thread with a tiny red strand in it. Everyone looked at it earnestly.

'Well – it *might* have been pulled out of the thief's jumper,' said Janet at last. 'We can all look out for somebody wearing a blue wool pullover with a tiny thread of red in it!'

And then they found something else – something *much* more exciting!

Seven

Scamper finds a clue

IT was really Scamper the spaniel who found the biggest clue of all. He was with them, of course, sniffing round eagerly, very interested in the curious round marks. Then he suddenly began to bark loudly.

Everyone looked at him. 'What's up, Scamper?' said Peter.

Scamper went on barking. The three girls felt a bit scared, and looked hastily round, half afraid that there might be somebody hidden in the bushes!

Scamper had his head up, and was barking quite madly. 'Stop it,' said Peter, exasperated. 'Tell us what you're barking at, Scamper! Stop it, I say.'

Scamper stopped. He gave Peter a reproachful look and then gazed up above the children's heads. He began to bark again.

Everyone looked up, to see what in the world the spaniel was barking at. And there, caught neatly on the twig of a tree, was a cap!

'Look at that!' said Peter, astonished. 'A cap! Could it belong to the thief?'

'Well, if it does, why in the world did he throw his cap up there?' said Janet. 'It's not a thing that thieves usually do – throw their caps up into trees and leave them!'

The cap was far too high to reach. It was almost as high up as the top of the wall! Mr Johns the gardener went to get a stick to knock it down.

'It could only have got up there by being thrown,' said George. 'So it doesn't really seem as if it could have belonged to the thief. He really wouldn't go throwing his cap about like that, leaving such a very fine clue!'

'No. You're right, I'm afraid,' said Peter. 'It can't be his cap. It must be one that some tramp threw over the wall some time or other.'

Mr Johns came back with a bamboo stick. He jerked the cap off the twig and Scamper pounced on it at once.

'Drop it, Scamper, drop it!' ordered Peter, and Scamper dropped it, looking hurt. Hadn't he spotted the cap himself? Then at least he might be allowed to throw it up into the air and catch it!

The Seven looked at the dirty old cap. It was made of tweed, and at one time must have showed a

rather startling check pattern – but now it was so dirty that it was difficult even to see the pattern. Janet looked at it in disgust.

'Ugh! What a dirty cap! I'm sure that some tramp had finished with it and threw it over the wall – and it just stuck up there on that tree branch. I'm sure it isn't a clue at all.'

'I think you're right,' said Colin, turning the cap over and over in his hands. 'We might as well chuck it over into Little Thicket. It's no use to us. Bad luck, Scamper – you thought you'd found a thumping big clue!'

He made as if to throw the cap up over the wall, but Peter stopped him. 'No, don't! We'd better keep it. You simply never know. We'd kick ourselves if we threw away something that might prove to be a clue of some kind – though I do agree with you, it probably isn't.'

'Well, *you* can carry the smelly thing then,' said Colin, giving it to Peter. 'No wonder somebody threw it away. It smells like anything!'

Peter stuffed it into his pocket. Then he took the tiny piece of blue wool thread, and put that carefully into the pages of his notebook. He looked down at the ground where the curious marks were.

'I almost think we'd better make a note of these too,' he said. 'Got a measure, Janet?'

She hadn't, of course. But George had some string, and he carefully measured across the round marks, and then snipped the string to the right size. 'That's the size of the marks,' he said, and gave his bit of string to Peter. It went carefully into his notebook too.

'I can't help thinking those funny marks all over the place are some kind of clue,' he said, putting his notebook away. 'But what, I simply can't imagine!'

They said goodbye to Mr Johns, and made their way home across the fields. Nobody could make much of the clues. Peter did hope the adventure wasn't going to fizzle out, after all!

'I still say that only an acrobat could have scaled that high wall,' said Janet. 'I don't see how any ordinary person could have done it!'

Just as she said this, they came out into the lane. A big poster had been put up on a wall nearby. The children glanced at it idly. And then Colin gave a shout that made them all jump!

'Look at that – it's a poster advertising a circus! And see what it says – Lion-tamers, Daring Horse-riders, Performing Bears – Clowns – and Acrobats! Acrobats! Look at that! Supposing – just supposing . . .'

They all stared at one another in excitement. Janet might be right. This must be looked into at once!

Eight

A visit to the circus

PETER looked at his watch. 'Bother!' he said in dismay. 'It's nearly dinner-time. We must all get back home as fast as we can. Meet at half-past two again, Secret Seven.'

'We can't!' said Pam and Barbara. 'We're going to a party.'

'*Don't* have a meeting without us,' begged Pam.

'I can't come either,' said George. 'So we'd better make it tomorrow. Anyway, if the thief *is* one of the acrobats at the circus, he won't be leaving this afternoon! He'll stay there till the circus goes.'

'Well – it's only just a *chance* he might be an acrobat,' said Janet. 'I only just *said* it could only be an acrobat that scaled that high wall. I didn't really mean it!'

'It's worth looking into, anyhow,' said Peter. 'Well – meet tomorrow at half-past nine, then. And will everybody please think hard, and have some kind of plan to suggest? I'm sure we shall think of something good!'

Everyone thought hard that day – even Pam and Barbara whispered together in the middle of their party! 'I vote we go and see the circus,' whispered Pam. 'Don't you think it would be a good idea? Then we can see if Peter recognises any of the acrobats as the thief he saw hiding under that bush!'

When the Secret Seven met the next day, muttering the password as they went through the door of the shed, everyone seemed to have exactly the same idea!

'We should visit the circus,' began George.

'That's just what Pam and I thought!' said Barbara.

'I thought so too,' said Colin. 'In fact, it's the only sensible thing to do. Don't you think so, Peter?'

'Yes. Janet and I looked in the local paper, and we found that the circus opens this afternoon,' said Peter. 'What about us all going to see it? I don't know if I would recognise any of the acrobats as the thief – I really only caught just a glimpse of him, you know – but it's worth trying.'

'You said he was dark and clean-shaven,' said Colin. 'And I saw that his hair was black, anyway.

He had a little thin patch on the top. But it isn't much to go on, is it?'

'Has anyone got any money?' asked Pam. 'To buy circus tickets, I mean? I haven't any at all, because I had to buy a birthday present to take to the party yesterday.'

Everyone turned out their pockets. The money was put in a pile in the middle and counted.

'The tickets are one pound for children,' said Peter with a groan. 'One pound! They must think that children are *made* of money. We've got four pounds here, that's all. Only four of us can go.'

'I've got two pounds in my money-box,' said Janet.

'And I've got ninety pence at home,' said Colin. 'Anyone got the odd ten pence?'

'Oh yes – I'll borrow it from Susie,' said Jack.

'Well, don't go and tell her the password in return for the money!' said Colin, and got a kick from Jack and an angry snort.

'Right. That looks as if we can all go, after all,' said Peter, pleased. 'Meet at the circus field ten minutes before the circus begins. Don't be late, anyone! And keep your eyes skinned for anyone wearing a dark blue pullover with a tiny thread of

red in it – because it's pretty certain the thief must have worn a jumper or pullover made of that wool.'

Everyone was very punctual. All but Pam had money with them, so Peter gave her enough for her ticket. They went to the ticket-box and bought seven tickets, feeling really rather excited. A circus was always fun – but to go to a circus and keep a look out for a thief was even more exciting than usual!

Soon they were all sitting in their seats, looking down intently on the sawdust-strewn ring in the middle of the great tent. The band struck up a cheerful tune and a drum boomed out. The children sat up, thrilled.

In came the horses, walking proudly, their feathery plumes nodding. In came the clowns, somersaulting and yelling; in came the bears; in came all the performers, one after another, greeting the audience with smiles.

The children watched out for the acrobats, but they were all mixed up with the other performers – five clowns and conjurers, two clever stilt-walkers, and five men on ridiculous bicycles. It was impossible to tell which were the acrobats.

'They are third on the programme,' said Peter.

'First come the horses – then the clowns – and then the acrobats.'

So they waited, clapping the beautiful dancing horses, and laughing at the ridiculous clowns until their sides ached.

'Now for the acrobats!' said Peter, excitedly. 'Watch, Colin, watch!'

Nine

A good idea – and a disappointment

THE acrobats came in, turning cart-wheels and springing high into the air. One came in with his body bent so far over backwards that he was able to put his head between his legs. He looked very peculiar indeed.

Peter nudged Colin. 'Colin! See that fellow with his head between his legs – he's clean-shaven like the man I saw hidden in the bush – and he's got black hair!'

Colin nodded. 'Yes – he may be the one! All the others have moustaches. Let's watch him carefully and see if he could really leap up a high wall, and over the top.'

All the Secret Seven kept their eyes glued on this one acrobat. They had seen that the others had moustaches, so that ruled them out – but this one fitted the bill – he was dark-haired and had no moustache!

Could he leap high? Would he show them that he could easily leap up a steep wall to the top? They watched eagerly. The clean-shaven acrobat was easily the best of them all. He was as light as a feather. When he sprang across the ring it almost seemed as if his feet did not even touch the ground.

He was a very clever tight-rope walker too. A long ladder was put up, and was fixed to a wire high up in the roof of the tent. The children watched the acrobat spring lightly up the ladder, and they turned to look at one another – yes – if he could leap up a ladder like that, hardly touching the rungs with feet or hands, he could most certainly leap up a twelve-foot wall to the top!

'I'm sure that one's the thief,' whispered Janet to Peter. He nodded. He was sure, too. He was so sure, that he settled down to enjoy the circus properly, not bothering to look out for a thief any longer, now that he had made up his mind this was the one.

It was quite a good circus. The performing bears came on, and really seemed to enjoy themselves boxing with each other and with their trainer. One little bear was so fond of its trainer that it kept hugging his leg, and wouldn't let him go!

Janet wished she had a little bear like that for a

pet. 'He's just like a big teddy,' she said to Pam, and Pam nodded.

The clowns came in again – and then the two stilt-walkers, with three of the clowns. The stilt-walkers were ridiculous. They wore long skirts over their stilts, so that they looked like tremendously tall people, and they walked stiffly about with the little clowns teasing them and jeering at them.

Then a strong cage was put up, and the lions were brought in, snarling. Janet shrank back. 'I don't like this,' she said. 'Lions aren't meant to act about. They only look silly. Oh dear – look at that one – he won't get up on his stool. I know he's going to pounce on his keeper.'

But he didn't, of course. He knew his perform-ance and went through it very haughtily with the others. They ambled away afterwards, still snarling.

Then a big elephant came in and began to play cricket with his trainer. He really enjoyed that, and when he hit the ball into the audience six times running, everyone clapped like mad.

Altogether, the children enjoyed themselves enormously. They were sorry when they found themselves going out into the big field again.

'If we could only hunt for thieves in circuses every time, it would be very enjoyable,' said Janet. 'Peter –

what do you think? Is that dark-haired, clean-shaven acrobat the thief? He's the only likely one of the acrobats, really.'

'Yes – all the others have moustaches,' said Peter. 'I wonder what we ought to do next? It would be a good thing, perhaps, to go and find him and talk to him. He might let something slip that would help us.'

'But what excuse can we give for going to find him?' said George.

'Oh – ask him for his autograph!' said Peter. 'He'll think that quite natural!'

The others stared at him in admiration. What a brainwave! Nobody had thought of half such a good idea.

'Look,' whispered Barbara. 'Isn't that him over there, talking to the bear-trainer? Yes, it is. Does he look like the thief to you, Peter, now that you can see him close?'

Peter nodded. 'Yes, he does. Come on – we'll all go boldly up and ask him for an autograph. Keep your eyes and ears open.'

They marched up to the acrobat. He turned round in surprise. 'Well – what do you want?' he asked with a grin. 'Want a lesson on how to walk the tightrope?'

'No – your autograph, please,' said Peter. He stared at the man. He suddenly seemed much older than he had looked in the ring. The acrobat laughed. He mopped his forehead with a big red handkerchief.

'It was hot in the tent,' he said. 'Yes, you can have my autograph – but just let me take off my wig first. It makes my head so hot!'

And, to the children's enormous surprise, he loosened his black hair – and lifted it off completely! It was a wig – and under it, the acrobat was completely bald. Well – *what* a disappointment!

Ten

Trinculo the acrobat

THE Seven stared at him in dismay. Why – his head was completely bald except for a few grey hairs right on the very top. He couldn't possibly be the thief. Colin had distinctly seen the top of the thief's head when he had sat above him in the tree – and he had said that his hair was black, except for a little round bald patch in the centre.

Colin took the wig in his hand. He looked at it carefully, wondering if perhaps the thief had worn the wig when he had stolen the necklace. But there was no little round bald patch in the centre! It was a thick black wig with no bare patches at all.

'You seem to be very interested in my wig,' said the acrobat, and he laughed. 'No acrobat can afford to be bald, you know. We have to look as young and beautiful as possible. Now, I'll give you each my autograph, then you must be off.'

'Thank you,' said Peter, and handed the man a piece of paper and a pencil.

The little bear came ambling by, all by itself, snorting a little.

'Oh, *look*!' said Janet in delight, 'Oh, will it come to us, do you think? Come here, little bear.'

The bear sidled up and rubbed against Janet. She put her arms round it and tried to lift it – but it was unexpectedly heavy. A strange, sulky-looking youth came after it, and caught it roughly by the fur at its neck.

'Ah, bad boy!' he said, and shook the little creature. The bear whimpered.

'Oh, don't!' said Janet in distress. 'He's so sweet. He only came over to see us.'

The youth was dressed rather peculiarly. He had on a woman's bodice, spangled with sequins, a bonnet with flowers in – and dirty flannel trousers!

Peter glanced at him curiously as he led the little bear away. 'Was he in the circus?' he asked. 'I don't remember him.'

'Yes – he was one of the stilt-walkers,' said the acrobat, still busily writing autographs. 'His name's Louis. He helps with all the animals. Do you want to come and see the bears in their cage some time? – they're very tame – and old Jumbo would love to have a bun or two if you like to bring him some. He's as gentle as a big dog.'

'Oh yes – we'd *love* to!' said Janet, at once thinking how much she would love to make friends with the dear little bear. 'Can we come tomorrow?'

'Yes – come tomorrow morning,' said the acrobat. 'Ask for Trinculo – that's me. I'll be about somewhere.'

The children thanked him and left the field. They said nothing till they were well out of hearing of any of the circus folk.

'I'm glad it wasn't that acrobat,' said Janet. 'He's nice. I like his funny face, too. I did get a shock when he took off his black hair!'

'So did I,' said Peter. 'I felt an idiot, too. I thought I had remembered how the thief had looked – when I saw Trinculo's face, I really did think he looked like the thief. But he doesn't, of course. For one thing, the man I saw was much younger.'

'We'd better not go by faces, it seems to me,' said Colin. 'Better try to find someone who wears a blue pullover with a red thread running through it!'

'We can't go all over the district looking for *that*,' said Pam. 'Honestly, that's silly.'

'Well, have you got a better idea?' asked Colin.

She hadn't, of course. Nor had anyone else. 'We're stuck,' said Peter, gloomily. 'This is a silly sort of mystery. We keep thinking we've got somewhere – and then we find we haven't.'

'Shall we go to the circus field tomorrow?' asked Pam. 'Not to try to find the thief, of course, because we know now that he isn't any of the acrobats. But should we go just to see the animals?'

'Yes. I did like that little bear,' said Janet. 'And I'd like to see old Jumbo close to, as well. I love elephants.'

'I don't think I'll come,' said Barbara. 'I'm a bit scared of elephants, they're so enormous.'

'I won't come, either,' said Jack. 'What about you, George? We said we'd swop stamps tomorrow, you know.'

'Yes – well, we won't go either,' said George. 'You don't mind, do you, Peter? I mean, it's nothing to do with the Society, going to make friends with bears and elephants.'

'Well, Janet and Pam and Colin and I will go,' said Peter. 'And mind – everyone is to watch out for a blue pullover with a little red line running through it. You simply *never* know what you'll see if you keep your eyes open!'

Peter was right – but he would have been surprised to know what he and Janet were going to spot the very next day!

Eleven

Pam's discovery

NEXT morning Janet, Peter, Colin and Pam met to go to the circus field. They didn't take Scamper, because they didn't think Jumbo the elephant would like him sniffing round his ankles.

He was very angry at being left, and they could hear his miserable howls all the way up the lane. 'Poor Scamper!' said Janet. 'I wish we could have taken him – but he might get into the lions' cage or something. He's so very inquisitive.'

They soon came to the field. They walked across it, eyeing the circus folk curiously. How different they looked in their ordinary clothes – not *nearly* so nice, thought Janet. But then, how exciting and magnificent they looked in the ring.

One or two of them had built little fires in the field and were cooking something in black pots over the flames. Whatever it was that was cooking smelt most delicious. It made Peter feel very hungry.

They found Trinculo, and he was as good as his

word. He took them to make friends with Jumbo, who trumpeted gently at them, and then, with one swing of his strong trunk, he set Janet high up on his great head. She squealed with surprise and delight.

They went to find the little bear. He was delighted to see them, and put his paws through the bars to reach their hands. Trinculo unlocked the cage and let him out. He lumbered over to them and clasped his arms round Trinculo's leg, peeping at the rest of them with a roguish look on his funny bear-face.

'If only he wasn't so *heavy*,' said Janet, who always loved to pick up any animal she liked and hug it. 'I wish I could buy him.'

'Goodness – whatever would Scamper say if we took him home?' said Peter.

Trinculo took them to see the great lions in their cages. The sulky youth called Louis was there with someone else, cleaning out the cages. The other man in the cage grinned at the staring children. One of the lions growled.

Janet backed away. 'It's all right,' said the trainer. 'They're all harmless so long as they are well fed, and don't get quarrelsome. But don't come too near, Missy, just in case. Here you, Louis. Fill the water-trough again – the water's filthy.'

Louis did as he was told. The children watched him tip up the big water-trough and empty out the dirty water. Then he filled it again. He didn't seem in the least afraid of the lions. Janet didn't like him, but she couldn't help thinking how brave he was!

They were all sorry when it was time to go. They said goodbye to Trinculo, went to pat the little bear once more, and then wandered across the field to Jumbo. They patted as far as they could reach up his pillar-like leg, and then went along by the row of bright caravans to the gate at the end of the field.

Some of the caravanners had been doing their washing. They had spread a good deal of it out on the grass to dry. Others had rigged up a rough clothes-line, and had pegged up all kinds of things to flap in the wind.

The children wandered by, idly looking at everything they passed. And then Pam suddenly stopped short. She gazed closely at something hanging on one of the lines. When she turned her face towards them, she looked so excited that the others hurried over to her.

'What is it?' asked Peter. 'You look quite red! What's up?'

'Is anybody looking at us?' asked Pam in a low voice. 'Well, Peter – hurry up and look at these socks hanging on this line. What do they remind you of?'

The others looked at the things on the line – torn handkerchiefs, little frocks belonging to children, stockings and socks. For a moment Peter felt sure that Pam had spotted a blue pullover!

But there was no pullover flapping in the wind. He wondered what had attracted Pam's attention. Then he saw what she was gazing at.

She was looking very hard indeed at a pair of blue wool socks – and down each side of them ran a pattern in red! Peter's mind at once flew to the scrap of wool he had in his pocket-book – did it match?

In a trice he had it out and was comparing it with the sock. The blue was the same. The red was the same. The wool appeared to be exactly the same too.

'And see here,' whispered Pam, urgently. 'There's a little snag in this sock – just here – a tiny hole where a bit of the wool has gone. I'm pretty certain, Peter, that that's where your bit of blue wool came from – this sock!'

Peter was sure of it, too. An old woman came up and shooed them away. 'Don't you dare touch those clothes!' she said.

Peter didn't dare to ask who the socks belonged to. But if only, only he could find out, he would know who the thief was at once!

Twelve

One-leg William

THE old circus woman gave Pam a little push. 'Didn't you hear me say go away!' she scolded. They all decided to go at once. Pam thought the old woman looked really rather like a witch!

They walked quickly out of the field, silent but very excited. Once they were in the lane they all talked at once.

'We never *thought* of socks! We thought we had to look for a pullover!'

'But it's socks all right – that pair is made of exactly the same wool as this bit we found caught on to that wall!'

'Gracious! To think we didn't dare to ask whose socks they were!'

'If only we had, we'd know who the thief was.'

They raced back to the farmhouse, longing to discuss what to do next. And down in the shed, patiently waiting for them, were Jack, George and Barbara! They didn't give the others a chance to tell about the socks – they immediately began to relate something of their own.

'Peter! Janet! You know those strange round marks we saw on the inside of the wall! Well, we've found some more, exactly like them!' said Jack.

'Where?' asked Peter.

'In a muddy patch near old Chimney Cottage,' said Jack. 'George and I saw them and went to fetch Barbara. Then we came to tell you. And what's more, Barbara knows what made the marks!'

'You'll never guess!' said Barbara.

'Go on – tell us!' said Janet, forgetting all about the socks.

'Well, when I saw the marks – round and regular, just like the ones we saw – I couldn't think what they were at first,' said Barbara. 'But then, when I remembered who lived in the nearby cottage, I knew.'

'What were they?' asked Peter, eagerly.

'Do you know who lives at Chimney Cottage?' asked Barbara. 'You don't. Well, I'll tell you – it's One-leg William! He had a leg bitten off once by a shark, and he's got a wooden leg – and when he walks in the mud with it, it leaves round marks – *just* like the marks we saw on the other side of the wall. It must be One-leg William who was the thief.'

The others sat and thought about this for a few moments. Then Peter shook his head.

'No. One-leg William couldn't possibly be the thief. He couldn't have climbed over the wall with one leg – and besides – the thief wore a pair of socks – and that means *two* legs!'

'How do you know he wore socks?' asked Barbara, astonished.

They told her about the socks on the line away in the circus field. Barbara thought hard.

'Well – I expect the thief *was* a two-legged man with socks – but I don't see why One-leg William couldn't have been with him to help in some way – give him a leg-up, or something. The marks are *exactly* the same! What was One-leg William doing there, anyway?'

'That's what we must find out,' said Peter, getting up. 'Come on – we'll go and ask him a few questions – and see those marks. Fancy them being made by a one-legged man – I never, never thought of that!'

They made their way to Chimney Cottage. Just outside was a very muddy patch – and sure enough, it was studded with the same round, regular marks that the children had seen over Milton Manor wall. Peter bent down to study them.

He got out his notebook and took from it the bit

of string that George had cut when he measured the width of the other round marks. He looked up in surprise.

'No – these marks *aren't* the same – they're nearly an inch smaller – you look!' He set the string over one of the marks, and the others saw at once that it was longer than the width of the marks.

'Well! Isn't that funny!' said George. 'It *couldn't* have been One-leg William, then. Is there another man with a wooden leg in the district? One whose leg might be a bit wider and fit the marks?'

Everyone thought hard – but nobody could think of a man with a wooden leg. It was really exasperating! 'We keep *on* thinking we're solving things, and we aren't,' said Peter. 'There's no doubt in my mind that a man with a wooden peg-leg was there with the thief, though goodness knows why – but it wasn't One-leg William. And we do know that the *thief* can't have only one leg because he definitely wears two socks!'

'We know his socks – but we don't know *him*!' said Janet. 'This mystery is getting more mysterious than ever. We keep finding out things that lead us nowhere!'

'We shall have to go back to the circus field tomorrow and try to trace those socks,' said Peter.

'We can't ask straight out whose they are – but we could watch and see who's wearing them!'

'Right,' said Colin. 'Meet there again at ten – and we'll have a squint at every sock on every foot in that field!'

Thirteen

A coat to match the cap

At ten o'clock all the Secret Seven were in the circus field. They decided to go and see Trinculo the acrobat again, as an excuse for being there. But he was nowhere to be found.

'He's gone off to the town,' said one of the other acrobats. 'What do you want him for?'

'Oh – just to ask him if we can mess around a bit,' said Jack. 'You know – have a squint at the animals and so on.'

'Carry on,' said the acrobat, and went off to his caravan, turning cart-wheels all the way. The children watched him in admiration. 'How *do* they turn themselves over and over their hands and feet like that?' asked Pam. 'Just exactly like wheels turning round and round!'

'Have a shot at it,' said George, with a grin. But when Pam tried to fling herself over on her hands, she crumpled up at once, and lay stretched out on the ground, laughing.

A small circus-girl came by, her tangled hair hanging over her eyes. She laughed at Pam, and immediately cart-wheeled round the field,. turning over and over on her hands and feet just as cleverly as the acrobat.

'Look at that,' said George, enviously. 'Even the kids can do it. We shall have to practise at home.'

They went to look at the little bear, who, however, was fast asleep. Then they wandered cautiously over to the clothes line. The socks were gone! Aha! Now perhaps someone was wearing them. Whoever it was would be the thief.

The children strolled round the field again, looking at the ankles of every man they saw. But to their great annoyance all they could see had bare ankles! Nobody seemed to wear any socks at all. How maddening!

Louis came up to the lions' cage and unlocked it. He went inside and began to do the usual cleaning. He took no notice of the lions at all, and they took no notice of him. Janet thought it must be marvellous to go and sweep all round the feet of lions and not mind at all!

He had his dirty flannel trousers rolled up to his knees. His legs, also dirty, were quite bare. On his feet were dirty old rubber shoes.

The children watched him for a little while, and then turned to go. Another man came up as they left, and they glanced casually down at his ankles, to see what kind of socks he wore, if any. He was bare-legged, too, of course!

But something caught Jack's eyes, and he stopped and stared at the man intently. The fellow frowned. 'Anything wrong with me?' he said, annoyed. 'Stare away!'

Jack turned to the others, his face red with excitement. He pushed them on a little, till he was out of the man's hearing.

'Did you see that coat he was wearing?' he asked. 'It's like that cap we found up in the tree – only not quite so filthy dirty! I'm sure it is!'

All seven turned to look round at the man, who was by now painting the outside of the lions' cage, making it look a little smarter than before. He had taken off his coat and hung it on the handle of the lions' cage. How the Seven longed to go and compare the cap with the coat!

'Have you got the cap with you?' asked Pam in a whisper. Peter nodded, and patted his coat pocket. He had all the 'clues' with him, of course!

Their chance suddenly came. The man was called away by someone yelling for him, and went off, leaving his paint-pot, brush and coat. Immediately the children went over to the coat.

'Pretend to be peering into the lions' cage while I compare the cap with the coat,' said Peter in a low voice. They all began to look into the cage and talk about the lions, while Peter pulled the cap out of his pocket and quickly put it against the coat.

He replaced the cap at once. There was no doubt about it – the cap and coat matched perfectly. Then

was this fellow who was painting the lions' cage the thief? But how did it happen that he had thrown his cap high up in a tree? Why did he leave it behind? It just didn't make sense.

The man came back, whistling. He stooped down to pick up his paint-brush, and Colin got a splendid view of the top of his head. He gazed at it.

Then all the children moved off in a body longing to ask Peter about the cap. Once they were out of hearing, he nodded to them. 'Yes,' he said. 'They match. That fellow *may* be the thief, then. We'll have to watch him.'

'No good,' said Colin, unexpectedly. 'I just caught sight of the top of his head. He's got black hair – but no round bare patch at the crown, like the man had who sat below me in that tree. *He's* not the thief!'

Fourteen

The peculiar marks again

THE Seven went to sit on the rails of the fence that ran round the circus field.

They felt disheartened.

'To think we find somebody wearing a coat that *exactly* matches the cap we found – and yet he can't possibly be the thief because the top of his head is wrong!' groaned Peter. 'I must say this is a most aggravating adventure. We keep finding out exciting things – and each time they lead us nowhere at all!'

'And if we find anyone wearing those socks that we are sure belong to the thief, it won't be him at all either,' said Janet. 'It will probably be his aunt, or something!'

That made everyone laugh. 'Anyway,' said Peter, 'we're not absolutely *certain* that the cap has anything to do with the theft of the necklace. We only found it flung high up in a tree, you know, near where the thief climbed over the wall.'

'It has got something to do with the mystery,' said George. 'I'm sure of it – though I can't for the life of me think how.'

They all sat on the fence and gazed solemnly over the field. What an annoying adventure this was! And then Janet gave a little squeal.

'What is it? Have you thought of something?' asked Peter.

'No. But I'm seeing something,' said Janet, and she pointed over to the right. The others looked where she pointed, and how they stared!

The field was rather wet just there, and in the damp part were round, regular marks just like those they had seen by the wall – and very like the smaller marks made by the one-legged man near his cottage!

'I think *these* marks are the right size,' said Peter, jumping down in excitement. 'They look bigger than the marks made by the one-legged man's wooden leg. I'll measure them.'

He got out his bit of string and laid it carefully across one of the marks. Then across another and another. He looked up joyfully.

'See that. Exactly the same size! Every one of these round marks is the same as those we saw in the ground below the wall the thief climbed!'

'Then – there must be another one-legged man here, in the circus – a man with a wooden leg that measures the same as those round marks,' said Colin, excitedly. 'He's not the thief, because a one-legged man couldn't climb the wall, but he must have been *with* the thief!'

'We must find him,' said George. 'If we can find who his friend is, or who he shares a caravan with, we shall know his friend is the thief – and I expect we'll find that the thief is wearing those socks, too! We're getting warmer!'

Peter beckoned to the small circus girl who had turned cart-wheels some time before. 'Hey, you!' he called. 'We want to talk to the one-legged man here. Which is his caravan?'

'Don't be daft,' said the small girl. 'There bain't no one-legged man here. What'd he be doing in a circus? All of us here have got our two legs – and need 'em! You're daft!'

'Now look here,' said Peter, firmly. 'We know there *is* a one-legged man here and we mean to see him. Here's some chocolate if you'll tell us where he is.'

The little girl snatched the chocolate at once. Then she laughed rudely, 'Chocolate for nothing!' she said. 'You're nuts! I tell you, there bain't no one-legged fellow here!'

And before they could ask her anything else, she was gone, turning over on hands and feet as fast as any clown in the circus!

'You run after her and catch her,' called a woman from a nearby caravan. 'But she won't tell you no different. We ain't got no one-leggy man here!'

She went into her caravan and shut the door. The Seven felt quite taken aback. 'First we find marks outside Chimney Cottage and are certain they belong to the thief,' groaned Peter, 'but they belong to a one-legged man who is nothing to do with this adventure – and then we find the *right* marks, right size and all – and we're told there isn't a one-legged man here at all! It's really very puzzling!'

'Let's follow the marks,' said Janet. 'We shall find them difficult to see in the longer grass – but maybe we can spot enough to follow them up.'

They did manage to follow them. They followed them to a small caravan parked not far from the lions' cage, next to a caravan where Louis was sitting on the steps. He watched them in surprise.

They went up the steps of the small caravan and peered inside. It seemed to be full of odds and ends of circus properties. Nobody appeared to live there.

A stone skidded near to them and made them jump. 'You clear off, peeping and prying where you've no business to be!' shouted Louis, and picked up another stone. 'Do you hear me? Clear off!'

Fifteen

A shock for Peter and Colin

THE Seven went hurriedly out of the circus field and into the lane. George rubbed his ankle where one of Louis's stones had struck him.

'Beast!' he said. 'Why didn't he want us to peep in that little old caravan? It's only used for storing things, anyway.'

'Maybe the thief has hidden the pearls there!' said Janet with a laugh.

Peter stared at her and thought hard. 'Do you know – you might be right!' he said, slowly. 'We are certain the thief belongs to the circus – we're certain the pearls must be there – and why should Louis be so upset when we just peeped into that caravan?'

'I wish we could search it and see,' said Colin, longingly. 'But I don't see how we can.'

'Well, *I* do!' said Peter. 'You and I will go to *tonight's* performance of the circus, Colin – but we'll slip out at half-time, when all the performers are in the ring, or behind it – and we'll see if those pearls *are* hidden there!'

'But surely they won't be?' asked Pam. 'It seems such a silly place.'

'I've got a sort of a hunch about it,' said Peter, obstinately. 'I just can't explain it. Those weird round marks seemed to lead there, didn't they? Well, that's peculiar enough, to begin with.'

'It certainly is,' said Barbara. 'Marks made by a one-legged man who doesn't exist! This is a silly adventure, I think.'

'It isn't really,' said George. 'It's a bit like a jigsaw puzzle – the bits look quite odd and hopeless when they're all higgledy-piggledy – but as soon as you fit them together properly, they make a clear picture.'

'Yes – and what we've got so far is a lot of odd bits that really belong to one another – a tweed cap that matches a coat worn by someone we know isn't the thief! Weird marks that turn up everywhere and don't tell us anything.'

'Come on – let's get home,' said Jack, looking at his watch. 'It's almost dinner-time. We've spent all the morning snooping about for nothing. Actually I'm beginning to feel quite muddled over this adventure. We keep following up trails that aren't any use at all.'

A shock for Peter and Colin

'No more meetings today,' said Peter, as they walked down the lane. 'Colin and I will meet tonight by ourselves and go to the circus. Bring a torch, Colin. Gosh – suppose we found the pearls hidden in that old caravan!'

'We shan't,' said Colin. 'I can't think why you're so set on searching it. All right – meet you at the circus gate tonight!'

He was there first. Peter came running up a little later. They went in together, groaning at having to pay out two pounds more. 'Just for half the show, too,' whispered Peter.

The two boys went into the big tent and found seats near the back, so that they could easily slip out unnoticed. They sat down and waited for the show to begin.

It really was very good, and the clowns, stilt-walkers and acrobats seemed better than ever. The boys were quite sorry to slip out before the show was over.

It was dark in the circus field now. They stopped to get their direction. 'Over there,' said Peter, taking Colin's arm. 'See – that's the caravan, I'm sure.'

They made their way cautiously towards the caravan. They didn't dare to put on their torches in

case someone saw them and challenged them. Peter fell over the bottom step of the caravan, and then began to climb up carefully.

'Come on,' he whispered to Colin. 'It's all clear! The door isn't locked, either. We'll creep in, and begin our search immediately!'

The two boys crept into the caravan. They bumped into something in the darkness. 'Dare we put on our torches yet?' whispered Colin.

'Yes. I can't hear anyone near,' whispered back Peter. So, very cautiously, shading the beam with their hands, they switched on their torches.

They got a dreadful shock at once. They were in the wrong caravan! This wasn't the little caravan in which all kinds of things from the circus were stored – this was a caravan people lived in. Good gracious! Suppose they were caught, what a row they would get into.

'Get out, quickly!' said Peter. But even as he spoke, Colin clutched his arm. He had heard voices outside! Then someone came up the step. Whatever *were* they going to do now!

Sixteen

Prisoners

'QUICK! Hide under that bunk thing – and I'll hide under this,' whispered Peter in a panic. He and Colin crawled underneath, and pulled the hangings over them. They waited there, trembling.

Two men came into the caravan, and one of them lit a lamp. Each sat down on a bunk. Peter could see nothing of them but their feet and ankles.

He stiffened suddenly. The man on the bunk opposite had pulled up his trouser legs, and there, on his feet, were the blue socks with the faint red lines running down each side!

To think he was sitting opposite the man who must be the thief – and he couldn't even see his face to know who it was! Who could it be?

'I'm clearing out tonight,' said one man. 'I'm fed up with this show. Nothing but grousing and quarrelling all the time. And I'm scared the police'll come along sooner or later about that last job.'

'You're always scared,' said the man with the

socks. 'Let me know when it's safe to bring you the pearls. They can stay put for months, if necessary.'

'Sure they'll be all right?' asked the other man. The man with the socks laughed, and said a most peculiar thing.

'The lions will see to that,' he said.

Peter and Colin listened, frightened and puzzled. It was plain that the thief was there – the man with the socks, whose face they couldn't see – and it was also quite plain that he had hidden the pearls away for the time being – and that the first man had got scared and was leaving.

'You can say I'm feeling too sick to go on again in the ring tonight,' said the first man, after a pause.

'I'll go now, I think, while everyone's in the ring. Get the horse, will you?'

The man with the socks uncrossed his ankles and went down the steps. Peter and Colin longed for the other fellow to go too. Then perhaps they could escape. But he didn't go. He sat there, drumming on something with his fingers. It was plain that he felt nervous and scared.

There were sounds outside of a horse being put between the shafts. Then the man with the socks called up the steps.

'All set! Come on out and drive. See you later.'

The man got up and went out of the caravan. To the boys' intense dismay he locked the door! Then he went quietly round to the front of the van, and climbed up to the driving seat. He clicked to the horse and it ambled off over the field.

'I say!' whispered Colin. 'This is awful! He locked that door! We're prisoners!'

'Yes. What a bit of bad luck,' said Peter, crawling out from his very uncomfortable hiding-place. 'And did you notice, Colin, that one of the men had those socks on! He's the thief. And he's the one we've left behind, worse luck.'

'We've learnt a lot,' said Colin, also crawling out. 'We know the pearls are somewhere in the circus. What did he mean about the lions?'

'Goodness knows,' said Peter. 'Unless he's put them into the lions' cage and hidden them somewhere there. Under one of the boards, I expect.'

'We'll have to escape somehow,' said Colin, desperately. 'Could we get out of a window, do you think?'

The boys peeped cautiously out of the window at the front, trying to see where they were. The caravan came to a bright street lamp at that moment – and Peter gave Colin a sharp nudge.

'Look!' he whispered. 'That fellow who's driving the caravan has got on the tweed coat that matches the old cap we found up in the tree. It must be the fellow we saw painting the outside of the lions' cage!'

'Yes. And probably the thief borrowed his cap to

wear, seeing that they live in the same caravan,' said Colin. 'That makes *one* of the bits of jigsaw pieces fit into the picture, anyway.'

They tried the windows. They were tightly shut. Colin made a noise trying to open the window and the driver looked back sharply into the van. He must have caught sight of the face of one of the boys by the light of a street lamp, for he at once stopped the horse, jumped down, and ran round to the back of the van.

'Now we're for it!' said Peter in despair. 'He's heard us. Hide quickly, Colin! He's unlocking the door!'

Seventeen

Back at the circus field

THE key turned in the lock and the door of the caravan was pushed open. A powerful torch was switched on, and the beam flashed round the inside of the van.

The boys were under the bunks and could not be seen. But the man was so certain that somebody was inside the van that he pulled aside the draperies that hung over the side of the bunk where Peter was hiding. At once he saw the boy.

He shouted angrily and dragged poor Peter out. He shook him so hard that the boy yelled. Out came Colin at once to his rescue!

'Ah – so there are two of you!' said the man. 'What are you doing here? How long have you been in this van?'

'Not long,' said Peter. 'We came in by mistake. We wanted to get into another van – but in the dark we missed our way.'

'A pretty poor sort of story!' said the man,

angrily. 'Now I'm going to give you each a good hiding – that will teach you to get into other people's caravans.'

He put down his torch on a shelf, so that its beam lighted the whole caravan. He pushed back his coat sleeves and looked very alarming indeed.

Colin suddenly kicked up at the torch. It jerked into the air and fell to the floor with a crash. The bulb was broken and the light went out. The caravan was in darkness.

'Quick, Peter, go for his legs!' yelled Colin, and dived for the man's legs. But in the darkness he missed them, shot out of the door, and rolled down the steps, landing with a bump on the road below.

Peter got a slap on the side of his head and dodged in the darkness. He, too, dived to get hold of the man's legs and caught one of them. The man hit out again and then staggered and fell. Peter wriggled away, half fell down the steps and rolled into the hedge.

At the same moment the horse took fright and galloped off down the road with the caravan swinging from side to side behind it in a most alarming manner. The man inside must have been very, very surprised indeed!

'Colin! Where are you?' shouted Peter. 'Come

on, quickly. The horse has bolted with the caravan and the man inside it. Now's our chance!'

Colin was hiding in the hedge, too. He stepped out to join Peter, and the two set off down the road as fast as they could, running at top speed, panting loudly.

'Every single thing in this adventure goes wrong,' said Colin at last, slowing down. 'We can't even get into the right caravan, when we want to – we have to choose the wrong one.'

'Well, we learnt quite a bit,' said Peter. 'And we know the thief is wearing those socks now, even if we still don't know who he is. Funny thing is – I seem to know his voice.'

'Have you any idea at all where we are?' asked Colin. 'I mean – do you suppose we're running *towards* home, or away from it? As this is a most contrary adventure, I wouldn't be surprised if we're running in the wrong direction as fast as ever we can!'

'Well, we're not,' said Peter. 'I know where we are all right. In fact, we'll soon be back at the circus field. I say – should we slip into the field again and just have a squint round for the man who's wearing the socks? I feel as if I simply *must* find out who he is!'

Colin didn't want to. He had had enough adventure for one night. But he said he would wait for Peter outside the gate if he badly wanted to go into the field again.

So Peter slipped over the fence and made his way to where he saw many lights. The show was over, and the people had gone home. But the circus folk were now having their supper, and the light from lanterns and fires looked very bright and cheerful.

Peter saw some children playing together. One of them appeared very tall indeed – and Peter saw that she was walking on stilts, just as the stilt-walkers did in the ring. It was the rude little girl who had told him there was no one-legged man in the circus. She came walking over to where he stood by a caravan, but she didn't see him. She was absorbed in keeping her balance on the stilts.

She came and went – and Peter stared at something showing on the ground. Where the child had walked, her stilts had left peculiar marks pitted in the ground – regular, round marks – just like the ones by the wall round Milton Manor! There they were, showing clearly in the damp ground, lit by the flickering light of a nearby lantern!

'Look at that!' said Peter to himself. 'We were *blind*! Those marks weren't made by a one-legged man – they were made by a stilt-walker! Why ever didn't we think of it before?'

Eighteen

Peter tells his story

PETER gazed down at the number of weird round marks. He looked over at the child who was stilt-walking – yes, everywhere she went, her stilts left those round marks on the ground. Now another bit of the jigsaw had fitted into place.

'The thief was a stilt-walker,' said Peter to himself. 'He took his stilts with him to help him get over the wall. I must find Colin and tell him!'

He ran over to where Colin was waiting for him. 'Colin, I've discovered something exciting!' he said. 'I know what makes those peculiar round marks – and they're nothing to do with a one-legged man!'

'What makes them then?' asked Colin, surprised.

'Stilts!' said Peter. 'The ends of stilts! The thief was on stilts – so that he could easily get over that high wall. What a very clever idea!'

'But how did he do it?' said Colin puzzled. 'Come on, let's go home, Peter. I shall get into an awful row, it's so late. I'm terribly tired, too.'

'So am I,' said Peter. 'Well, we won't discuss this exciting evening any more now – we'll think about it and have a meeting tomorrow morning. I'll send Janet round for the others first thing. As a matter of fact, I haven't *quite* worked out how the thief did climb over the wall with stilts.'

Colin yawned widely. He felt that he really could not try to think out anything. He was bruised from his fall out of the caravan, he had banged his head hard, and he felt rather dazed. All he wanted to do was to get into bed and go to sleep!

Janet was fast asleep when Peter got home, so he didn't wake her. He got into bed, meaning to think everything out carefully – but he didn't, because he fell sound asleep at once!

In the morning he wouldn't tell Janet a word about the night's adventures. He just sent her out to get the others to a meeting. They came, wondering what had happened. One by one they hissed the password – 'Adventure!' – and passed through the door. Colin was last of all. He said he had overslept!

'What happened last night? Did you find the pearls? Do you know who the thief is?' asked Pam, eagerly.

'We didn't find the pearls – but we know everything else!' said Peter, triumphantly.

'*Do* we!' said Colin, surprised. 'You may, Peter – but I don't. I still feel sleepy!'

'Peter, tell us,' said George. 'Don't keep us waiting. Tell us everything!'

'Come on up to Little Thicket and I'll show you exactly how the thief got over that wall,' said Peter, suddenly deciding that that would be a very interesting way of fitting all the bits of the jigsaw together.

'Oh – you *might* tell us now!' wailed Janet, bitterly disappointed.

'No. Come on up to Little Thicket,' said Peter. So they all went together to Little Thicket, and walked over to the big gates of Milton Manor. Mr Johns the gardener was there again, working in the front beds of the drive.

'Mr Johns! May we come in again?' shouted Peter. 'We won't do any harm.'

Mr Johns opened the gates, grinning. 'Discovered anything yet?' he asked as the children crowded through.

'Yes, lots,' said Peter, and led the way to the place where the thief had climbed over the wall. 'Come along with us and I'll tell you what we've discovered, Mr Johns!'

'Right – but I'll just let this car in at the gates

first,' said Mr Johns, as a big black car hooted outside.

The children soon came to the place where they had been before. 'Now look,' said Peter, 'this is what happened. The thief was a stilt-walker, so all he had to do was to come to the outside of this wall,

get up on his stilts – walk to the wall, lean on the top, take his feet from the stilts and sit on the wall. He then draws his stilts over the wall and uses them on this soft ground. On the hard garden paths they don't mark, and he is safe to come to earth and hide his stilts along the box hedging of the border.'

'Go on!' said Janet in excitement.

'He gets into the house, takes the pearls, and comes back to the wall,' said Peter. 'Up he gets on his stilts again and walks to the wall – and he leaves more of these peculiar round stilt-marks behind in the earth, of course!'

'Goodness – *that's* what they were!' said Pam.

'Yes. And as he clambers on to the wall, his cap catches a high branch of a tree and is jerked off,' said Peter. 'He leaves it there because he doesn't want to waste time getting it back. He catches one of his socks on that little sharp piece of brick and leaves a bit of wool behind . . . then he's up on the top of the wall, and down he jumps on the other side!'

'Which I heard him do!' said Colin. 'But, Peter – he had no stilts when I saw him. *What did he do with his stilts?*'

Nineteen

Where are the pearls?

'You want to know what he did with the stilts he used when he climbed up on the wall after he had stolen the pearls?' said Peter. 'Well – I don't really know – but if all my reasoning is right, he must have flung them into a thick bush, somewhere, to hide them!'

'Yes – of course,' said Pam. 'But which bush?'

They all looked round at the bushes and trees near by. 'A holly bush!' said Colin, pointing over the wall. 'That's always so green and thick, and people don't go messing about with holly because it's too prickly!'

'Yes – that would certainly be the best,' said Peter. 'Come on, everyone.' He led the rest out of the Manor grounds and round to the other side of the wall at top speed.

They were soon finding out what a very scratchy, prickly job bending back the branches of the thick holly tree could be. But what a reward they had!

There, pushed right into the very thickest part, were two long stilts! Colin pulled out one and Peter pulled out the other.

'You were right, Peter!' said Janet. 'You *are* clever! We've explained simply everything now – the old cap high up on a branch – the bit of wool – the peculiar round marks – how the thief climbed an unclimbable wall. Really, I think the Secret Seven have been very, very clever!'

'And so do I!' shouted another voice. They all turned, and there, flushed and breathless, was their friend the inspector of police, with Mr Johns the gardener still a good ten yards off.

'Hello!' said Peter, surprised. 'I say – did you hear that?'

'Yes,' said the inspector, beaming but breathless. 'Mr Johns here opened the gate to my car, and told me he thought you had solved the mystery. We knew you must be hot on the scent of something when you chased out of the gate like that. Well, what's your explanation? You've certainly beaten the police this time!'

Peter laughed. 'Ah well, you see – we can go snooping about the circus without anyone suspecting us – but if you sent seven policemen to snoop round the circus field, you'd certainly be suspected

of something!'

'No doubt we should,' agreed the inspector. He picked up the stilts and examined them. 'A very ingenious way of scaling an enormously high wall. I suppose you can't also tell me who the thief is, can you?'

'Well – it's a stilt-walker, of course,' said Peter. 'And I *think* it's a fellow called Louis. If you go to the circus you'll probably find him wearing blue socks with a little red thread running down each side.'

'And he'll have black hair with a little round bare place at the crown,' said Colin. 'At least – the thief *I* saw had a bare place there.'

'Astonishing what a lot you know!' said the inspector, admiringly. 'You'll be telling me the colour of his pyjamas next! What about coming along to find him now? I've got a couple of men out in the car. We can all go.'

'Oooh,' said Pam, imagining the Secret Seven appearing on the circus field with three big policemen. 'I say – won't the circus folk be afraid when they see us?'

'Only those who have reason to be afraid,' said the inspector. 'Come along. I do want to see if this thief of yours has a bare place on the crown of his

head. Now, *how* do you know that, I wonder? Most remarkable!'

They all arrived at the circus field at last. The police got there first, of course, as they went in their car, but they waited for the children to come. Through the gate they all went, much to the amazement of the circus folk there.

'There's Louis,' said Peter, pointing out the sullen-looking young fellow over by the lions' cage. 'Bother – he's got no socks on again!'

'We'll look at the top of his head then,' said Colin.

Louis stood up as they came near. His eyes looked uneasily at the tall inspector.

'Got any socks on?' inquired the inspector, much to Louis's astonishment. 'Pull up your trousers.'

But, as Peter had already seen, Louis was bare-legged. 'Tell him to bend over,' said Colin, which astonished Louis even more.

'Bend over,' said the inspector, and Louis obediently bent himself over as if he were bowing to everyone.

Colin gave a shout. 'Yes – that's him all right! See the bare round patch at the crown of his head? Just like I saw when I was up in the tree!'

'Ah – good,' said the inspector. He turned to Louis again. 'And now, young fellow, I have one more thing to say to you. Where are the pearls?'

Twenty

The end of the adventure

LOUIS stared at them all sullenly. 'You're mad!' he said. 'Asking me to pull up my trouser legs, and bend over – and now you start talking about pearls. What pearls? I don't know nothing about pearls – never did.'

'Oh yes, you do,' said the inspector. 'We know all about you, Louis. You took your stilts to get over that high wall – didn't you? – the one that goes round Milton Manor. And you got the pearls, and came back to the wall. Up you got on to your stilts again, and there you were, nicely on top, ready to jump down the other side.'

'Don't know what you're talking about,' mumbled Louis sulkily, but he had gone very pale.

'I'll refresh your memory a little more then,' said the inspector. 'You left stilt marks behind you – and this cap on a high branch – and this bit of wool from one of your socks. You also left your stilts behind you, in the middle of a holly bush. Now, you didn't do all those things for nothing. Where are those pearls?'

'Find 'em yourself,' said Louis. 'Maybe my brother's gone off with them in the caravan. He's gone, anyway.'

'But he left the pearls here – he said so,' said Peter, suddenly. 'I was in the caravan when you were talking together!'

Louis gave Peter a startled and furious glance. He said nothing.

'And *you* said the pearls would be safe with the lions!' said Peter. 'Didn't you?'

Louis didn't answer. 'Well, well!' said the inspector. 'We'll make a few inquiries from the lions themselves!'

So accompanied by all the children, and the two policemen, and also by about thirty interested circus folk, and by the little bear who had somehow got free and was wandering about in delight, the inspector went over to the big lions' cage. He called for the lion-keeper.

He came, astonished and rather alarmed.

'What's your name?' asked the inspector. 'Riccardo,' replied the man. 'Why?' 'Well, Mr Riccardo, we have reason to believe that your lions

are keeping a pearl necklace somewhere about their cage or their persons.'

Riccardo's eyes nearly fell out of his head. He stared at the inspector as if he couldn't believe his ears.

'Open the cage and go in and search,' said the inspector. 'Search for loose boards or anywhere that pearls could be hidden.'

Riccardo unlocked the cage, still looking too astonished for words. The lions watched him come in, and one of them suddenly purred like a cat, but much more loudly.

Riccardo sounded the boards. None was loose. He turned, puzzled, to the watching people. 'Sir,' he said, 'you can see that this cage is bare except for the lions – and they could not hide pearls, not even in their manes – they would scratch them out.'

Peter was watching Louis's face. Louis was looking at the big water-trough very anxiously indeed. Peter nudged the inspector.

'Tell him to examine the water-trough!' he said.

Riccardo went over to it. He picked it up and emptied out the water. 'Turn it upside down,' called the inspector. Riccardo did so – and then he gave an exclamation.

'It has a false bottom soldered to it!' he cried. 'See, sir – this should not be here!'

He showed everyone the underneath of the water-trough. Sure enough, someone had soldered on an extra piece, that made a most ingenious false bottom. Riccardo took a tool from his belt and levered off the extra bottom.

Something fell out to the floor of the cage. 'The pearls!' shouted all the children at once, and the lions looked up in alarm at the noise. Riccardo passed the pearls through the bars of the cage, and then turned to calm his lions. The little bear, who was now by Janet, grunted in fear when he heard the lions snarling. Janet tried to lift him up, but she couldn't.

'Very satisfactory,' said the inspector, putting the magnificent necklace into his pocket. The children heard a slight noise, and turned to see Louis being marched firmly away by the two policemen. He passed a clothes-line – and there again were the blue socks, that had helped to give him away, flapping in the wind!

'Come along,' said the inspector, shooing the seven children in front of him. 'We'll all go and see Lady Lucy Thomas – and *you* shall tell her the story of your latest adventure from beginning to end.

119

She'll want to reward you – so I hope you'll have some good ideas! What do *you* want, Janet?'

'I suppose,' said Janet, looking down at the little bear still trotting beside her, 'I suppose she wouldn't give me a little bear, would she? One like this, but smaller so that I could lift him up? Pam would like one, too, I know.'

The inspector roared with laughter. 'Well, Secret Seven, ask for bears or anything you like – a whole circus if you want it. You deserve it. I really don't know what I should do without the help of the S.S.S.! You'll help me again in the future, won't you?'

'Rather!' said the Seven at once. And you may be sure they will!

ENID BLYTON'S:

THE SECRET ISLAND
THE SECRET OF SPIGGY HOLES
THE SECRET OF MOON CASTLE
THE SECRET MOUNTAIN
THE SECRET OF KILLIMOOIN